KU-502-988

CONTENTS

CHAPTER 1

It was dawn in the Viking village of Snortwik.

In the longhouse of Magnus Bigbelli, Grandma Grumpit stood by the fire and stirred a big pot of porridge. Her porridge came in five different kinds –

1. grey and gooey

2. grey and sticky

3. grey and slurpy

4. grey and lumpy

5. grey and drippy.

This morning it was the grey and gooey kind. Young Vigi wasn't eating it. He was flicking it. He put big dollops on his spoon and flicked them at the spiders that hung from the roof. His aim was good. He had knocked down five already.

Now Vigi put an extra big dollop on his spoon and aimed at an extra big spider. The porridge hit the spider and the spider fell to the ground.

Well, it fell *towards* the ground but it didn't *hit* the ground. In fact, it fell down Grandma Grumpit's neck. For an old lady Grandma Grumpit was very fast on her feet. In a second she had grabbed Vigi by the ear and pulled him to his feet.

"Ow!" Vigi screamed. "That's no way to treat a Viking warrior!"

"Warrior, my foot!" said Grandma. "You're just a messy, vulgar, little boy!"

Grandma dragged Vigi over to a bucket of water in the corner of the room. She dipped a cloth into the bucket and gave his face a wipe.

"Have you forgotten it's Parents' Day at school today?" she demanded as she took out her comb and tugged it through his hair.

"Your parents are waiting," she snapped.

Just then, a lump of porridge fell from the roof and hit her on the nose.

Vigi ran for the door as fast as he could.

CHAPTER 2

Vigi's mum and dad – Freda and Magnus Bigbelli – were standing outside. His mum was fussing over his dad's clothes. She pinned his best cloak round his neck with a silver pin. She tied his sword to his belt. She combed his fine, long beard. She polished his helmet. Last of all, she handed him his shield and axe.

"You're not going into battle, Dad," Vigi said. "You're just going to see my teacher."

"A Viking warrior must always look his best at times like this," said Magnus Bigbelli.

"Awwww! There's my lovely little boy!" said Freda. She came over to Vigi and gave him a big hug.

"Aw, Ma, get off!" said Vigi. "That's no way to treat a Viking warrior!"

"Viking warrior – you? We'll see what your teacher says about that!" said Magnus Bigbelli. "Let's go!"

He climbed up onto his horse. The horse walked ten steps then Magnus Bigbelli got off again. The school *was* just next door.

Magnus Bigbelli strode in to the school-house and threw his axe and shield on the table. This made Schoolmaster Skwirm wake up with a jump.

"Well, Schoolmaster?" Magnus Bigbelli bellowed. Schoolmaster Skwirm jumped again.

"Tell me," boomed Bigbelli. "How is my son Vigi doing at his lessons?"

"I ... er ... umm ..." the nervous schoolmaster stuttered. "I have his report card here."

He went over to a shelf where lots of bits of wood were stacked in a pile. He picked up at least a dozen pieces before he found the right one. He handed it to Bigbelli.

"Mmmm ... ar ... hmmm, excellent, excellent!" said Bigbelli as he peered at the marks scratched on the wood. Vigi took the piece of wood from him.

"Dad can't read," he told the schoolmaster. He read out the runes on the wood himself –

Reading – Good
Writing – Good
Singing – Very Good
Harp-Playing – Very Good
Wood Work – Excellent

"What good is all that?" Magnus Bigbelli bellowed. "None of that will turn him into a Viking warrior! Can he shout a war cry loud enough to make the enemy jump out of their boots?"

Schoolmaster Skwirm started to shake.

"Can he run wearing full armour and not break out in a sweat?" Magnus Bigbelli barked.

Schoolmaster Skwirm shook even more.

"Can he row a longship all morning without a break?" Magnus Bigbelli blared, banging his hand on the table. Schoolmaster Skwirm shook so much that he tripped over his bits of wood and fell over.

"I want to see a better report card next time," Bigbelli yelled. "You could start by giving your pupils some proper rowing practice." He turned to Vigi. "You couldn't tell an oar from a tooth pick!"

"Yes, I could!" said Vigi. "I am a Viking warrior! Watch me!"

"Oh, put a sock in it!" snarled Bigbelli. He picked up his shield and axe and marched out.

CHAPTER 3

Next morning, Grandma Grumpit dragged Vigi from his bed again.

"Hurry up, you horrid little boy. You'll be late for school!"

"That's no way to speak to a Viking warrior," moaned Vigi.

"If you're a Viking warrior, I'm a beauty queen," said Grandma. "Eat your porridge!"

This was a new type of porridge Vigi had never seen before. It was *yellow* and gloopy.

"I'm not really hungry, thanks," said Vigi. He pulled on his clothes and rushed out of the door.

Hirta and Olli, the other two pupils in Snortwick school, were already there when Vigi arrived.

Schoolmaster Skwirm was wearing a cloak and woolly hat.

"Today we are going to learn to row," he said.

"Oh, n-o-o-o!" moaned the Snortwick pupils.

"Silence!" said Schoolmaster Skwirm.
"Follow me!"

The Schoolmaster led his pupils down to the
harbour and pointed to a rowing boat tied up
nearby.

"Get in!" he said. "Pick up your oars!"

The pupils did as they were told.
Schoolmaster Skwirm got into the back of the
boat.

"We are going to row to One Sheep Island and back. Start rowing after I count to three. One! Two! Three!"

The pupils dug their oars into the water. They pulled and pulled and PULLED. The boat didn't move even a duck's foot from the shore.

"Useless! Useless!" shouted Schoolmaster Skwirm.

"I think you have to untie the boat first," said Vigi.

Schoolmaster Skwirm looked round and saw the boat was still tied to a post.

"Er, yes, I knew that," he said. "I was just testing your muscle power."

He untied the rope.

"Off we go! One! Two! Three!"

The pupils of Snortwick School dug their oars into the water again and off they went. They didn't row very fast. They didn't row very straight. The boat went to the left. It went to the right. Then it went round in a circle.

By the time they reached One Sheep Island, they were all tired out. Schoolmaster Skwirm had fallen asleep.

Vigi looked back across at the harbour. He saw his dad's beautiful longship, the *Wave Worm*.

He saw his dad standing beside the ship. He saw a man standing beside his dad.

The man walked round *Wave Worm*. He poked at it here and there. He came back to Magnus Bigbelli and they both shook hands.

Vigi didn't like the look of the man at all. Something wasn't right.

"Quick!" he yelled at Hirta and Olli. "Row back to the beach – as fast as you can!"

"But we've only just got here," Olli moaned.

"There's something fishy going on over there," said Vigi.

The pupils of Snortwick School pulled on their oars again with all their strength. The boat sped across the bay. It hit the beach with such a thump that Schoolmaster Skwirm toppled backwards into the water.

Vigi leaped out and ran along the beach to the *Wave Worm*.

"What's happening?" he yelled to Magnus Bigbelli.

Magnus was looking very pleased with himself. He pointed to the other man.

"This is Sigurd Sharpnose of *Sigurd's Super Ships*," he said. "He's offered me a good deal on a new ship."

"But there's nothing wrong with *our* ship," said Vigi.

Sigurd Sharpnose shook his head. "You've got slits in your sails. You've got worms in your wood. You've got barnacles on your bottom. If it's not leaking now it will be pretty soon. I'm offering you the *Golden Flier* instead – the fastest ship you'll ever sail."

21

"And what'll happen to *Wave Worm?*" Vigi asked.

"I'll take it off your hands," Sharpnose said.

"Nooooo!" Vigi shouted.

"Now off you go, you horrible little boy!" Magnus Bigbelli boomed. "We're doing an important deal here."

"It's a deal, then?" Sharpnose asked.

"It's a deal!" said Magnus Bigbelli.

They shook hands again.

"Put the cows, sheep, pigs and trousers on *Wave Worm* tonight," said Sharpnose. "I'll take the ship away first thing tomorrow morning and leave the *Golden Flier* in its place."

CHAPTER 4

That night, when everyone in the longhouse was asleep, Vigi sneaked out of bed. He lifted a bucket of Grandma Grumpit's porridge from beside the fire and slipped out of the door. He carried the porridge down to the beach and climbed on board the *Wave Worm*.

"Goodbye, old girl," Vigi said. He patted the carved head at the front of the ship. "I've brought you some of Grandma's porridge. I hope we'll meet again."

Then Vigi jumped down onto the sand.
He ran along to the other end of the beach,
climbed over a rock and crawled under some
bushes. Hidden back here was an old boat shed.
It was Vigi's secret place. He pushed open the
door and went in. He had something important
to do.

Next morning, a horrible noise rose up from the beach at Snortwick.

The noise came from Magnus Bigbelli. He was not happy. He marched up and down the sand like a bear with a sore head. No – like a bear with a sore head *and* toothache. *And* midges biting his backside.

"Just look at this!" he yelled at his crew of brave Viking warriors. The brave Viking warriors looked at his new ship, the *Golden Flier*.

They saw woodworm on the wood. They saw patches on the sails. They saw frayed ropes. They saw a VERY dodgy-looking ship indeed.

"I've been done!" Magnus Bigbelli yelled.
"I've been swindled! This ship isn't a *Golden Flier* – it's just *old and tired*!"

The brave Viking warriors laughed at Magnus Bigbelli's joke.

"Silence, idiots!" Bigbelli yelled. "When I catch Sigurd Sharpnose I'm going to ... I'm going to ... I'm going to feed him to the seagulls. What am I going to do?"

"Feed him to the seagulls!" said Bori Baldface.

"Feed him to the seagulls!" said Nafi Piksnot.

"Feed him to the seagulls!" said Floki Flatfeet.

"Lead him to the flea hills!" said Bolli Badbreath, who always got hold of the wrong end of the stick.

"So what are we waiting for?" Bigbelli yelled. "Let's go find him!"

They pushed the old and tired *Golden Flier* into the water and set off across the sea.

CHAPTER 5

Magnus Bigbelli had been yelling so much that he hadn't noticed the strange noises coming from the *other* end of Snortwick Bay that morning. There were bangs and crashes and thumps. The noises came from Vigi's boat-shed. He had been in there all night.

When at last Vigi came out, he saw the *Golden Flier*. It was far away and not moving very fast.

Vigi shook his head. "Oh dear, oh dear!" he muttered. "There's no time to lose!"

He crawled under the bushes, over the rock and along the bay.

Hirta and Olli were just about to go into school.

"Stop!" shouted Vigi. "I need you to come with me."

"But what about school?" Olli asked.

"Oh, Schoolmaster Skwirm will never notice," said Vigi.

The three of them peered in the door. Schoolmaster Skwirm was snoring loudly behind his desk.

"When he wakes up we'll tell him we've been doing rowing practice," said Vigi. "Come on, I've something to show you!"

He took them along the bay to the old boat-shed.

"There! What do you think of that?" he asked, with a proud grin.

Olli and Hirta looked at the strange thing that was sitting in the water. It was made of wood. It had lots of ropes. It had oars. It was like a ship but not a ship.

"Where did that come from?" Hirta asked.

"I built it," said Vigi. "It's a new kind of ship. It's called the *Dream Dragon*."

"It looks like a very *bad* dream," Hirta said. "Who's going to sail in it?"

"We are," said Vigi.

"I'm not rowing that thing," said Olli.

"Don't worry. You won't have to," Vigi told him. "Yuppi Yellowteeth is going to do the rowing. Let's go and get him now."

CHAPTER 6

Yuppi Yellowteeth was a horse. He was a horrible horse. He had long, yellow teeth. In fact, they were long yellow-grey-greenish teeth. He also liked to stick out his big wet tongue. The tongue went 'shlurpshlurpshlurp' against his long teeth and his big hairy lips. If you happened to be looking at him when he did that, you would go all queasy inside.

In spite of being horrible, Yuppi had lots of fans. These were the hundreds of little flies that liked his company.

Vigi led Yuppi Yellowteeth out of the field and down to his boat-shed. He pulled the horse onto the *Dream Dragon* and tied him to a post.

"Hirta, I want you to get up on Yuppi Yellowteeth's back and start riding when I tell you," said Vigi.

"But where am I riding to?" Hirta asked.

"You'll find out soon," said Vigi. He picked
up two poles and handed one to Olli. "I'm going
to untie the ship now," he said. "Then we'll push
it away from the shore with the poles."

Vigi untied the rope. He and Olli pushed
with their poles. The *Dream Dragon* floated
away from the shore.

"Right, Hirta, get trotting!" Vigi yelled.

"Giddie-up!" said Hirta, and she dug her heels into Yuppi Yellowteeth's sides. The horse began to trot but he didn't go anywhere. It was the floor under his feet that moved.

It went round and round.

The whole ship seemed to be dancing. Bits of wood went up and down. Bits of rope went *twang!* Wheels turned. As they turned, they made oars turn, too.

The *Dream Dragon* began to move forward.

"Wow!" said Hirta.

"Wow!" said Olli. "What do we do now?"

"We find Sigurd Sharpnose and we get *Wave Worm* back," said Vigi.

"But how do we find him?" Olli asked.

"We follow Grandma's porridge," said Vigi. "I hid a bucket of porridge on board the *Wave Worm*. The bucket has a hole in it. The porridge will slowly drip out and leave a trail in the water. You can't miss Grandma's porridge, it's ..."

"I think I can see it!" said Hirta from high on Yuppi Yellowteeth's back. "There's something in the sea up ahead."

Vigi and Olli ran to look. There was a lump of yellow stuff bobbing around in the sea. It looked like a very, very, ugly jellyfish.

"That's it!" yelled Vigi. "Come on, Olli, we must steer the ship!"

The two boys grabbed hold of the steering oar.

"Follow that porridge!" yelled Vigi.

CHAPTER 7

The trail of porridge led them past rocks and bays and islands. At last there was only one island left in all the sea. They drew closer and closer to it. The trail of porridge led right towards it.

"I think it's the place they call Dragon Island," Vigi said.

"We can't go there," said Hirta.

"They say a monster lives on it," said Olli.

Vigi shook his head. "Monster or not," he said, "we have to find *Wave Worm*."

They sailed close to the shore. It was not a pretty sight.

A gloomy mist drifted to and fro. Sharp rocks jutted out the water like sharks' teeth. There were wrecked ships everywhere. In the sky the birds swooped like witches.

Vigi peered through the mist.

"I can see *Wave Worm*!" he cried. "Over there, in that bay."

"Now what?" Hirta asked.

"Let's sail into the next bay," said Vigi.

They inched the *Dream Dragon* along between the rocks and into the next bay. Vigi jumped off the ship and onto a flat rock.

"Now what?" Olli asked.

"You wait here while I go and deal with Sharpnose!" said Vigi.

"On your own?" Hirta said. "You can't!"

But Vigi had already run off.

He scrambled over the rocks and into the next bay. He hid behind a big rock and peered

round it. Sharpnose was sitting by a bonfire
and looking very pleased with himself.

Vigi grabbed a stick, jumped out from his
hiding place and ran down the beach.

"I am a Viking warrior!" he yelled. "Watch
out! Watch out!"

Sharpnose turned round. For a second he
frowned, but then he smiled a crafty smile. Vigi
screeched to a halt.

'Oops!' he thought. 'Sharpnose can't sail a ship on his own. He must have ... a ... CREW.'

All of a sudden Vigi was surrounded by Vikings. Really ugly Vikings.

One had a scar across a cheek. Another had a grin full of rotten teeth. A third stared from just one eye and a fourth had a face full of boils. It was Gizor the Grim and his crew.

"Well, look who's here!" said Sigurd Sharpnose.

"Have you come to take your daddy's ship back from us?" Gizor the Grim sneered.

"It's all yours," said Black Tooth Barni.

"Just take it away!" said One Eye Erik.

"Safe journey!" said Lump-face Leif.

Then all the pirates hollered with laughter.

"Take him to the ship and tie him up!" said Gizor the Grim. "We'll keep him as a hostage."

"We can sell him back to his daddy for five horses," Sigurd Sharpnose said.

Vigi kicked and shouted and struggled, but it didn't do much good. They dragged him to *Wave Worm* and tied him to the mast. Then the pirates went back to their seats by the fire.

Vigi tried to wiggle free of the ropes. Just as he got tired of wiggling, he saw two faces appear over the side of the ship.

It was Hirta and Olli.

"We heard you shouting," said Hirta.

"So we came to rescue you," said Olli.

"Thanks for that," said Vigi. "But we need to scarper!"

Hirta and Olli clambered on to the ship. Just as they undid the last knot on Vigi's ropes, the Vikings spotted them.

"Run!" yelled Vigi. "Run back to the *Dream Dragon* and get ready to leave. I'll delay Gizor and his mob!"

Hirta and Olli slipped away into the mist.

CHAPTER 8

Vigi looked round the deck and grabbed a piece of wood. He stepped forward to a bucket. It was the bucket of Grandma's nasty porridge and there was still a little bit left.

Vigi scooped a lump up on his stick. If he could hit a spider, he could hit a Viking. He took aim. He fired.

A blob of Grandma's porridge flew through the air.

Splat!

It hit Black Tooth Barni right between the eyes.

"Uh?" grunted Black Tooth Barni, and grabbed at the gooey stuff on his face with his fingers.

Now, Grandma's porridge was not easy to get rid of. Black Tooth's fingers stuck to his face. He couldn't see where he was going any more. He spun round and crashed into Lump-face Leif. The two Vikings landed in a heap on the ground.

Splut!

Another blob of porridge flew through the air. It hit One Eye Erik's trousers. His legs stuck together and he toppled face down into the sand.

Gizor the Grim had almost reached *Wave Worm*. Splat! Splot! Splut! Splurp!

Lumps of porridge rained onto the beach behind him.

Vigi leaped down from the ship and raced back to the other bay. Hirta and Olli were already on board the *Dream Dragon*.

"Gizor and his mob are in a sticky situation," said Vigi. "But they'll be along soon. Let's get going!"

Vigi and Olli grabbed the wooden poles and pushed the *Dream Dragon* away from the rocks. Hirta climbed up on Yuppi Yellowteeth's back ready to get trotting.

But things didn't quite go to plan. Yuppi Yellowteeth's fan club of little flies was about to be joined by the flies of Dragon Island. The flies of Dragon Island were big, ugly, mean and hungry for blood. Just as *Dream Dragon* sailed out of the bay, Yuppi met his fan club's new members.

Yuppi Yellowteeth didn't like being bitten on the backside by an army of flies. He wanted to get home. He wanted to get home at a gallop. It was full speed ahead.

The *Dream Dragon* began to lurch from side to side.

"Stop him! Stop him!" yelled Vigi.

"I can't! I can't!" Hirta yelled back.

Vigi and Olli hung onto the steering oar for dear life.

The ship almost crashed into a rock that looked like a shark's tooth. It just missed another one. It swerved round a third.

"Look out! We're going to crash!" Hirta yelled.

The *Dream Dragon* hit one of the wrecked ships with a loud bang. The wreck's sail fell from its mast and landed on top of the *Dream Dragon*. Vigi, Olli and Hirta couldn't see a thing. Yuppi Yellowteeth's head stuck out through a hole in the sail. The horse was more spooked than ever.

Dream Dragon drifted onwards, towards the bay where Gizor the Grim and his gang were busy picking their teeth with their swords and looking out to sea.

Out of the mist came a hideous creature. It had a huge, lumpy body covered in grey, wrinkly skin. It had wild, rolling eyes. It had horrible yellow teeth. It had flippers that whirled round and round.

The Viking's jaws dropped open.

"What's ... what's ... *that?*" stammered Black Tooth Barni.

"It's the Monster of Dragon Island!" shrieked Lump-face Leif.

"To the ship! To the ship!" yelled Gizor.

The Vikings ran towards *Wave Worm* but the Monster of Dragon Island moved closer to *Wave Worm*, too.

"Run! Run for your lives!" yelled Gizor.

The Vikings turned and began to run the other way.

At last, Vigi, Olli and Hirta escaped from under the sail.

"Look!" said Hirta. "The Vikings are running away."

"Watch out!" yelled Vigi. "There's a huge rock right in front of us ..."

CRAAASSSSH!

The *Dream Dragon* hit the rock.

"Help!" said Olli. "*Dream Dragon* is falling to bits under our feet!"

"And the Vikings are running back towards us!" said Hirta.

"But *Wave Worm* is drifting towards us, too!" said Vigi. "Get ready to abandon ship! Everyone aboard *Wave Worm* NOW!"

As *Wave Worm* passed by, Vigi and Olli jumped. Hirta and Yuppi Yellowteeth jumped. Everyone landed safely on board.

"Now what do we do?" asked Olli.

"We row all the way home," said Vigi.

"WHAT!" shrieked Olli and Hirta together.

"Only joking," said Vigi. "The wind is blowing the right way. We can hoist the sail and it'll take us all the way back to Snortwick.

As they sailed away, they saw Gizor the Grim jumping up and down with rage on the beach. Vigi danced along the deck and sang ...

"I am a warrior Viking!
Watch me! Watch me!
If that's not to your liking,
then catch me! Catch me!"

He gave Gizor the Grim a wave.

CHAPTER 9

They were almost home when Hirta spotted something on a nearby island.

"There are some Vikings on that island!" she called. "They're waving at us."

"We don't want any more Viking trouble," said Vigi. "We'll just keep going."

Then Yuppi Yellowteeth gave a happy snort.

"I think he knows who these Vikings are," said Hirta.

Vigi stared hard at the island.

"It's my dad and his crew!" he said. "Steer for the island!"

Magnus Bigbelli was standing with his mouth open as *Wave Worm* drew in to the shore.

"Well, I never!" said Magnus Bigbelli. "It's *Wave Worm*!" He turned to his crew. "Do you see who's here?"

"Vigi, Olli and Hirta are here!" cheered Bori Baldface.

"Vigi, Olli and Hirta are here!" yelled Nafi Piksnot.

"Vigi, Olli and Hirta are here!" laughed Floki Flatfeet.

"Stick holly in a shirt, my dear!" said Bolli Badbreath who always got confused.

"What are *you* all doing here?" asked Vigi.

"That horrible old ship Sigurd Sharpnose sold me sprung a leak and sank," said Bigbelli. "We were marooned on this island. But what are *you* doing here?"

"We went to find Sigurd Sharpnose," said Vigi.

"On a ship that wasn't a ship," said Hirta.

"Yuppi Yellowteeth did the rowing," said Olli.

"Then I fought off Gizor the Grim and his mob," said Vigi.

"With the help of Grandma Grumpit's porridge," said Olli.

"Enough! Enough!" said Magnus Bigbelli. "You kids do my head in with your silly nonsense! I don't care how you got your hands on *Wave Worm* but you can help to row her back home."

"Am I a Viking warrior now?" asked Vigi.

"You'll be a Viking warrior when you can tie a bow in your beard!" bellowed Magnus Bigbelli. "Now get rowing!"

Our books are tested
for children and young people by
children and young people.

Thanks to everyone who consulted on
a manuscript for their time and effort in
helping us to make our books better
for our readers.